Jeremiah Learns to Read

by **Jo Ellen Bogart**

illustrated by **Laura Fernandez**
and **Rick Jacobson**

Orchard Books • New York

SPR JUN 3 - 2000

PUBLISHER'S NOTE

The United States Department of Education recently estimated that 21 to 23 percent of Americans sixteen and older are "functionally illiterate." These Americans struggle with everyday tasks such as understanding a bus schedule, reading directions on bottles of medicine, filling out simple forms—even reading road signs while driving.

If you know an adult who can't read but wants to learn how, you can help by contacting Literacy Volunteers of America for information about a chapter in your community. Their address is:

Literacy Volunteers of America
635 James Street
Syracuse, NY 13203-2214

Phone: (315) 472-0001
E-mail: info@literacyvolunteers.org
Web address: http://www.literacyvolunteers.org

Text copyright © 1997 by Jo Ellen Bogart
Illustrations copyright © 1997 by Laura Fernandez and Rick Jacobson
First American edition 1999 published by Orchard Books
First published in Canada in 1997 by North Winds Press, a division of Scholastic Canada Ltd.

Orchard Books, A Grolier Company, 95 Madison Avenue, New York, NY 10016

Manufactured in the United States of America
Printed and bound by Phoenix Color Corp. Book design by Mina Greenstein
The text of this book is set in 18 point Minion Semibold.
The illustrations are oil paintings.

10 9 8 7 6 5 4 3 2 1

Library of Congress Cataloging-in-Publication Data
Bogart, Jo Ellen.
Jeremiah learns to read / by Jo Ellen Bogart ; illustrated by Laura Fernandez and Rick Jacobson.—1st American ed.
p. cm.
Summary: Elderly Jeremiah decides that it's finally time to learn to read.
ISBN 0-531-30190-7 (trade : alk. paper).—ISBN 0-531-33190-3 (lib. bdg. : alk. paper)
I. Fernandez, Laura, ill. II. Jacobson, Rick, ill. III. Title.
PZ7.B635786 Je 1999 [E]—dc21   98-54913

For those who are learning the joys of reading

— J.E.B.

This book is dedicated to those, young and old,
who are learning to read, including our children,
Michael, Maite, and Mercedes.
A wonderful world will open up to you!

—L.F. and R.J.

Jeremiah knew how to build a split-rail fence, and he knew how to make buttermilk pancakes, but he didn't know how to read.

Jeremiah knew how to make a table out of a tree or make sweet syrup from its sap, but he didn't know how to read.

Jeremiah knew how to grow beautiful tomatoes, long green cucumbers, and juicy cobs of corn. He knew the tracks of the animals and the signs of the seasons, but he didn't know how to read letters and words.

"I want to learn to read," he said to his brother, Jackson, one day.

"You're an old man, Jeremiah," said Jackson. "You have children and grandchildren, and you can do almost anything."

"But I can't read," said Jeremiah.

"Well, you can learn, I suppose," said his brother. "But Jeremiah, who is going to teach you?"

"I want to learn to read," Jeremiah said to his wife, Juliana, that evening.

"You're just wonderful the way you are," said Juliana, as she worked on her knitting.

"But I can be even better," he said.

"Fine," said his wife. "I know you can learn. Then you can read to me." She smiled at him.

"I want to learn to read," Jeremiah said to his old sheepdog. The old dog just looked at him, then lay down on the rag rug by Jeremiah's feet.

"But how will I learn?" Jeremiah said. "My brother can't teach me. My wife can't teach me. And you, old friend, can't teach me either. How will I learn?"

Jeremiah thought and thought, feeling discouraged. But then an idea came to him, and his face broke out into a broad smile.

The next day, Jeremiah got up at sunrise and did all his morning chores. Then he washed his hands and his face, combed his hair and his beard, and put on his favorite shirt. He made biscuits and gravy with sliced tomatoes for breakfast and packed a sandwich for his lunch. Then he kissed Juliana good-bye and walked out the door.

He joined a group of children walking down the
tree-shaded lane. When they went into the schoolhouse, Jeremiah
went in too. Mrs. Trumble smiled with surprise when she saw him.

"I want to learn to read," he told her. Mrs. Trumble pointed at
an empty seat, and Jeremiah sat down.

"Class," she said, "we have a new student today. Please welcome
Jeremiah."

Jeremiah started by learning the letters and the sounds they made. Jeremiah tried hard, especially with the vowels. The children helped him practice at recess. And to thank them, he showed them how to chirp like a chickadee and honk like a goose.

Soon Jeremiah was learning to read words. He studied his lessons carefully. He practiced his writing every day.

Jeremiah loved it when the teacher and the older children read aloud to the class. Sometimes he drew pictures to go along with the stories while he listened.

Jeremiah was learning, but he was teaching too. He showed the Miller twins how to whittle with a pocketknife. He taught Mrs. Trumble how to make applesauce and how to whistle through her teeth.

After a while, Jeremiah was putting words together and writing his own stories. He wrote about the time he saved a baby squirrel. He wrote about swimming in the river with his brother, Jackson. He wrote about the day he met his wife.

Juliana watched Jeremiah practice his writing at the table after supper one night. "When are you going to read to me?" she asked him.

"When the time is right," he answered.

One day, Jeremiah took a book of poems home from school. Jeremiah hid the book under his pillow. That night, when he and Juliana went to bed, he pulled it out and showed it to her.

"Listen," he said.
He read a poem about
the soft petals and
sweet smell of roses.
He read a poem about
the crashing waves at
the seashore. He read
a poem about love.

Juliana looked into her husband's gray eyes. "Oh Jeremiah," she said. "I want to learn to read."

Jeremiah smiled at Juliana. "First thing after breakfast, my love." And Jeremiah turned off the light.